Follow the Line . . .

words
and
art
by

Laura Ljungkvist

VIKING

to an early morning in the big city,

How many clocks are there?

How many flowers
can you count?

How many TV antennas are there?

How many fire hydrants do you see?

How many orange buildings can you count?

where all the people just woke up...

How many striped shirts can you count?

How many babies do you see?

How many people have freckles?

How many people have curly hair?

How many hats do you see?

through the noisy traffic,

How many boxes are there on the red truck?

How many ambulances do you see?

with all the signs and lights ...

How many traffic lights are there?

How many of the signs are shaped like a triangle?

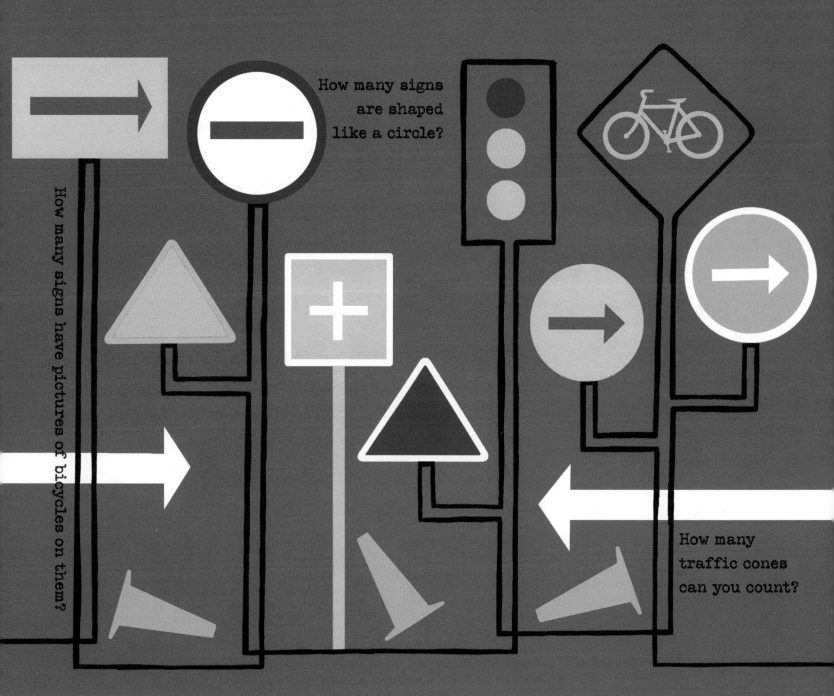

How many signs
are shaped
like a circle?

How many signs have pictures of bicycles on them?

How many
traffic cones
can you count?

across the wide ocean...

How many anchors can you count?

How many sailboats have striped sails?

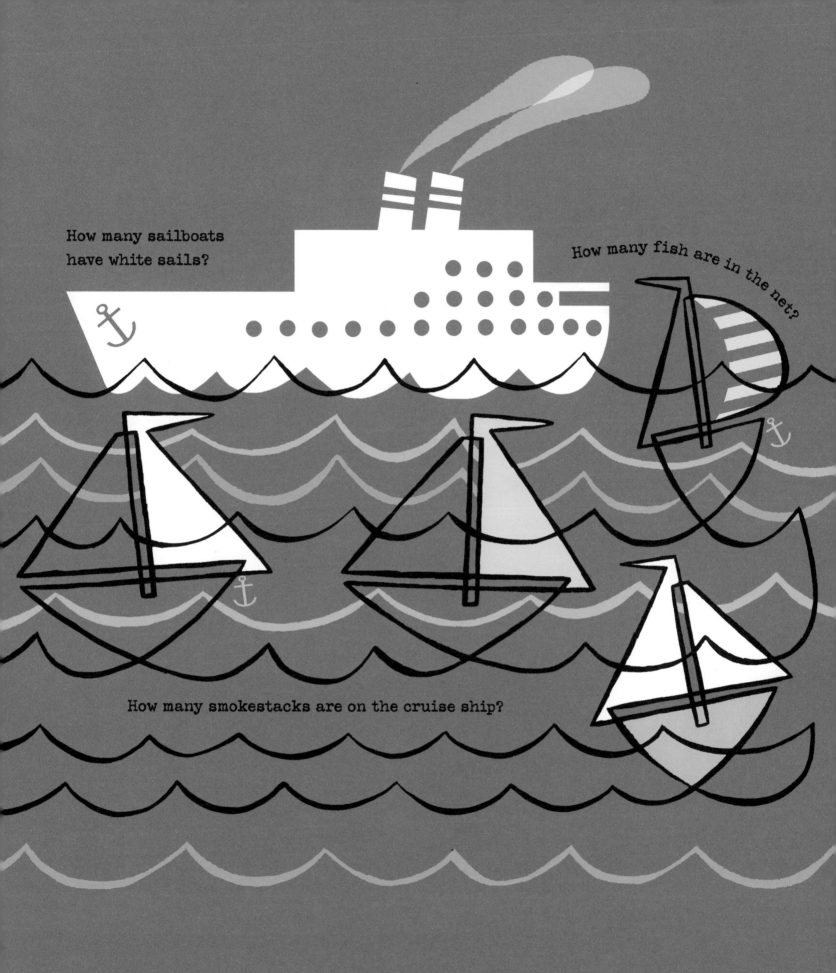

How many sailboats have white sails?

How many fish are in the net?

How many smokestacks are on the cruise ship?

deep under the water...

How many seashells can you count?

How many starfish do you see?

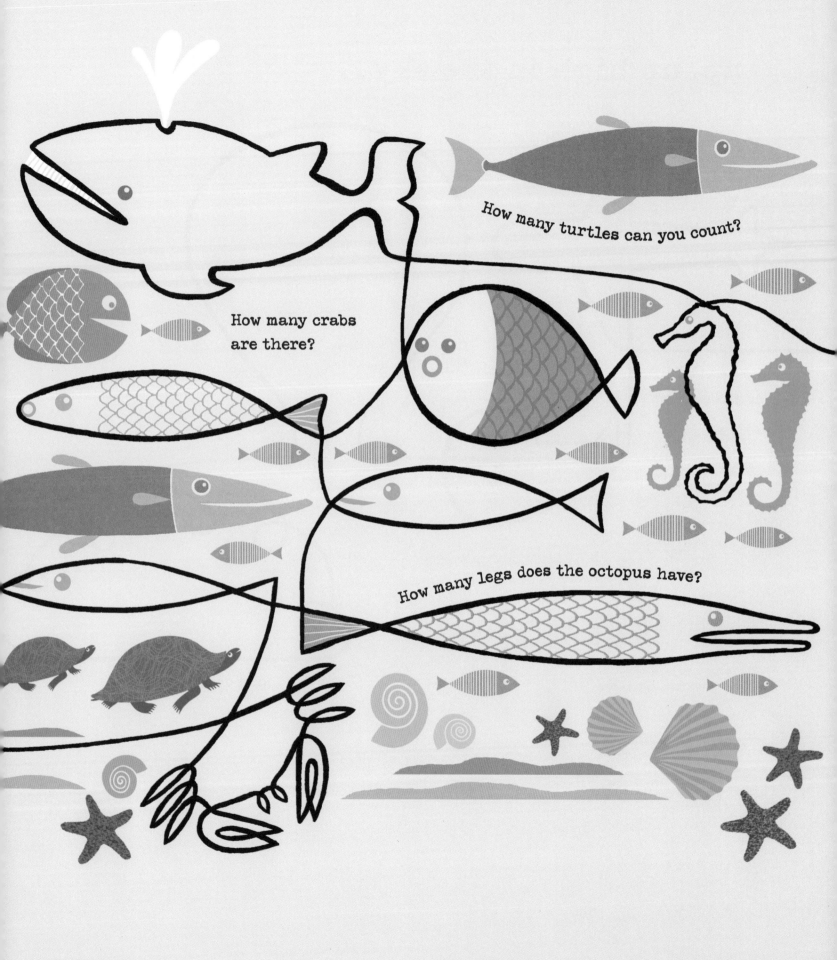

How many turtles can you count?

How many crabs are there?

How many legs does the octopus have?

up, up high in the sky . . .

How many birds
can you count?

How many balloons do you see?

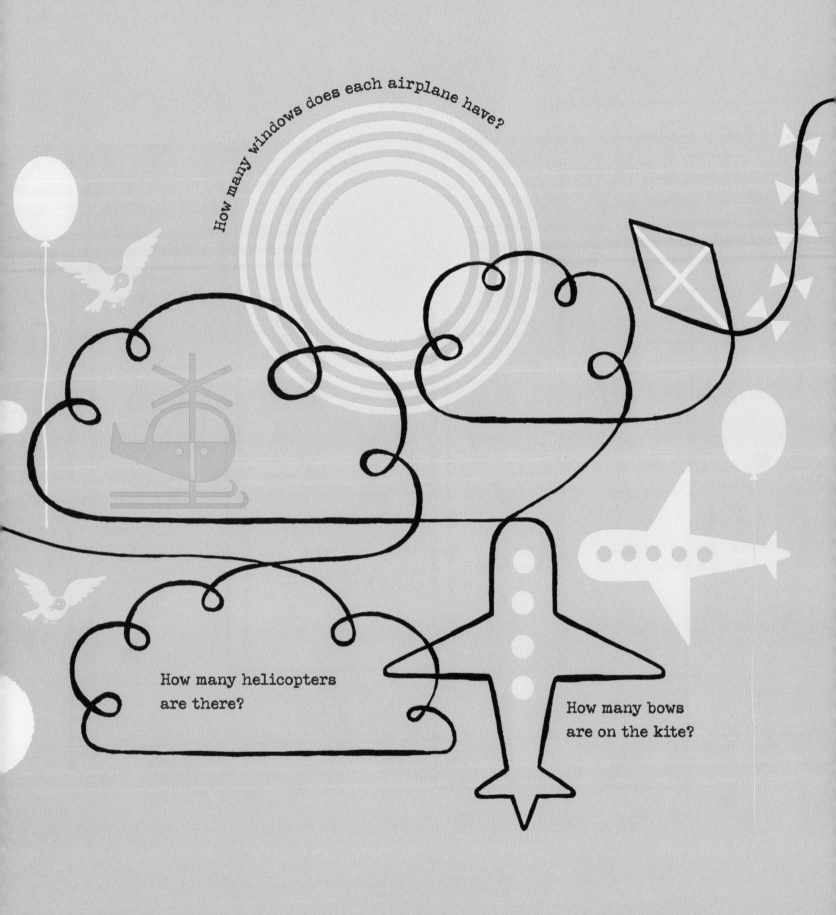

How many windows does each airplane have?

How many helicopters are there?

How many bows are on the kite?

into the big forest,

How many fallen trees do you see?

How many water lilies are in the pond?

How may pinecones do you see?

How many mushrooms can you count?

How many tree stumps are there?

where all the animals live...

How many dragonflies are there?

How many bats do you see?

How many bunnies can you count?

How many snails can you count?

How many snakes are there?

to the little country village...

How many blades does the windmill have?

How many fences are there?

How many houses have smoking chimneys?

How many tulips can you count?

How many doghouses do you see?

through the garden, to the little house,

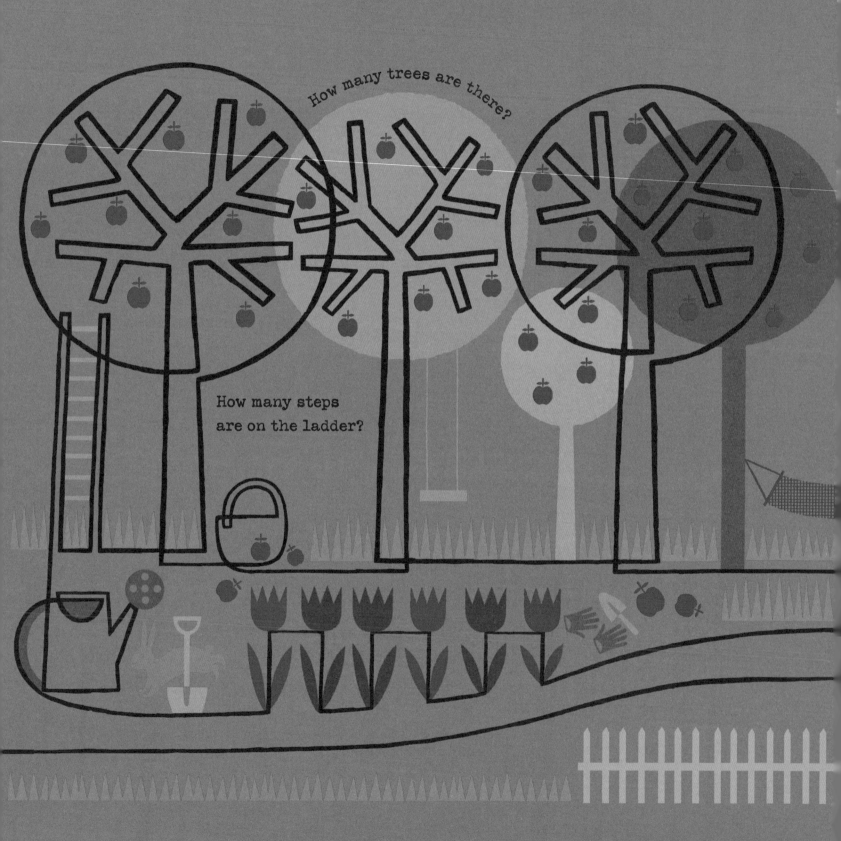

How many trees are there?

How many steps are on the ladder?

How many shirts are on the clothesline?

How many windows do you see on the house?

How many apples have fallen to the ground?